MARGARET K. McELDERRY BOOKS
An imprint of Simon & Schuster Children's Publishing Division
1230 Avenue of the Americas, New York, New York 10020
Copyright © 2015 by Ellie Sandall
Originally published in 2015 in Great Britain
by Hodder Children's Books
First U.S. edition 2016
MARGARET K. McELDERRY BOOKS is a trademark of
Simon & Schuster, Inc.
For information about special discounts for bulk purchases,
please contact Simon & Schuster Special Sales at 1-866-506-1949
or business@simonandschuster.com.
The Simon & Schuster Speakers Bureau can bring authors to your
live event. For more information or to book an event, contact the
Simon & Schuster Speakers Bureau at 1-866-248-3049 or visit
our website at www.simonspeakers.com.
The text for this book was set in Fiddlestix.
Manufactured in China
1215 HCB
10 9 8 7 6 5 4 3 2 1
CIP data is available from the Library of Congress.
ISBN 978-1-4814-7147-3 (hardcover)
ISBN 978-1-4814-7151-0 (eBook)

Ellie ✳ Sandall

Follow Me!

Margaret K. McElderry Books   New York   London   Toronto   Sydney   New Delhi

It's time to wake up!
Come down from the tree.

Follow me,

follow me,

follow me!

Places to be,

things to do, things to see.

Follow me, follow me, follow me!

things to chase,

Things to hunt,

things to race,

things to scare,

Follow me,

follow me,

follow me!

Things to climb, things to meet,

things to find,

things to eat.

Follow me,
follow me,
follow me!

Things to chew,

things to munch,

things to have
for our lunch.

Follow me,

follow me,

follow me!

Things to jump, things to hop, things to leap, things to . . .